Sandy

Michelle Medeiros

# SLEEPY RONALD

Written by JACK GANTOS    Illustrated by NICOLE RUBEL

1976

HOUGHTON MIFFLIN COMPANY BOSTON

# TO ERIC

**Library of Congress Cataloging in Publication Data**

Gantos, John B
  Sleepy Ronald.

  SUMMARY:  Ronald, usually a very alert and
lively rabbit, cannot stay awake until his friends
recognize his problem.
  [1.  Rabbits--Fiction.  2.  Sleep--Fiction]
I.  Rubel, Nicole.  II.  Title.
PZ7.G15334Sℓ    [E]        76-13599
ISBN 0-395-24743-8

Ronald was the most wide-awake rabbit
in his neighborhood.
He was always on the go.
In school he had lots of answers and on the
playground he was always full of fun.

But one morning  Ronald had a terrible time
getting out of bed.
He was so sleepy he couldn't even take
off his pajamas.
He fell asleep while brushing his teeth
and again while scrubbing his paws.
Not even his favorite breakfast of carrot
crunchies could keep him awake.

He could not pay attention in school.

Whenever his teacher wrote a problem on the blackboard Ronald fell asleep.

"What's wrong with Ronald?" Woodrow whispered to Possum.

"I don't know," said Possum, "but he'll never learn anything in his sleep."

After school Ronald climbed all the

way out to the tip of the high diving board.

"Hurry up and jump," yelled Priscilla.

"Get a move on," shouted Moose.

"He sure is slow," said Woodrow.

Then Ronald stretched out on the diving

board and fell sound asleep.

"Ronald certainly is acting odd,"

said Possum.

At the school dance everyone was having a great

time except Ronald.

He just sat on the stage and watched.

"Why don't you dance with someone?" asked Priscilla.

"Don't you like the music?" asked Woodrow.

"I'll join you in a minute," replied Ronald.

But in less than a minute he fell fast asleep.

The next day Ronald invited his friends
over for coleslaw and carrot juice.
When they arrived they found Ronald
asleep in his chair.
"How rude," sneered Possum.
"Ronald is no fun," huffed Priscilla.
"I'm insulted!" snapped Woodrow.
They left Ronald's house saying the nastiest
things about him.

The following evening Ronald was invited
to a party at Woodrow's house.

Ronald brushed his fur and put on his cap,
but when he crawled under his bed to find
his shoes he fell sound asleep.

Woodrow was terribly upset when Ronald
didn't arrive.

"There certainly is something wrong
with Ronald," he thought.

On Saturday when Ronald woke up he was so sleepy

he couldn't think of anything to do.

"I'll bet everyone else is having a great time,"

he thought. "I wish I could stay awake.

Maybe a cold bath will help."

But when he climbed into the tub he fell

fast asleep.

That afternoon Ronald slept right through

his opera rehearsal.

All of his friends agreed that he was positively

the rudest rabbit they knew.

"We are going to have to do something

about Ronald," exclaimed Priscilla.

"He ruins everything," Woodrow said sadly.

"Let's go wake him up," suggested Possum.

Everyone agreed and they marched over

to Ronald's house.

Ronald was asleep when his friends arrived.

They pounded on the door until he woke up.

"Why do you sleep all the time?" asked Priscilla.

"We haven't seen you in days," said Moose.

"We needed you for the rehearsal," added Woodrow.

"I don't know why I sleep all the time,"

answered Ronald. "I don't mean to spoil the fun.

I wish I could stay awake."

"Well, you'll just have to do something
about it," said Possum.

"Maybe it's because you wear your pajamas
all the time," suggested Moose.

"Let's get some clothes and see if that
will keep you awake."

They gathered all the different clothes they
could find and helped Ronald put them on.
But in only a minute his head leaned against
the chair and he fell sound asleep.

"Wake up! Wake up!" Woodrow shouted,

shaking Ronald.

"The best way for you to stop sleeping

all the time is to wear your roller skates."

"No one can sleep with roller skates on,"

said Priscilla.

"I agree." Possum nodded.

Ronald put on his roller skates

and was soon speeding down the street.

But the very next moment he was fast asleep.

Ronald was still sleeping when

Woodrow and Priscilla pushed him home.

Possum woke him up.

"There's no hope," Ronald said sleepily.

"I just can't stay awake."

"I have an idea," said Woodrow.

"No one can stand tickling.

That should keep you awake."

So they all tickled him.

Ronald giggled once or twice and

promptly fell asleep.

Then Priscilla stood behind Ronald

and placed her mouth just beneath one of his ears.

"BOO! BOO! BOO!"

she shouted so loud everyone jumped.

Ronald's ears popped straight up in the air.

"I'm wide awake!" he yelled.

He rubbed the sleep from his eyes.

"It's your ears!" yelled Priscilla.

"My ears?" asked Ronald.

"Yes, your ears. They keep drooping

over your eyes and make everything so dark

that you think it's bedtime."

"You solved the mystery," said Woodrow.

"Hooray!" shouted Possum.

Ronald was really quite amazed

and very, very happy.

"This calls for a celebration," announced Ronald.

They all went over to their favorite spot.

"We sure are having a good time," said Possum.

"You're a great guy, Ronald," said Woodrow.

"Now that you're awake," added Moose.

"You're the life of the party," said Priscilla.

It was late when Ronald waved good night

to all his friends. "See you tomorrow," he shouted.

Ronald could hardly wait to spend the next day

wide awake. He went home and climbed into bed.

His ears slowly drooped over his eyes

and he quietly fell asleep.

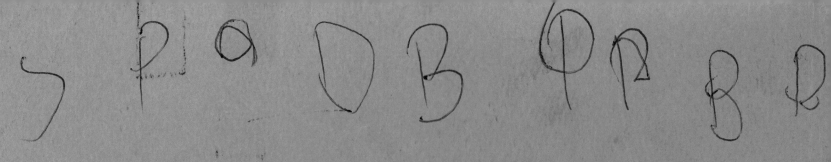